BEWARE!

PAULINE CARTWRIGHT

illustrated by
Annabel Craighead

LEARNING
MEDIA®

Distributed in the United States of America by Pacific Learning,
P.O. Box 2723, Huntington Beach, CA 92647-0723
Web site: www.pacificlearning.com

Published 1999 by Learning Media Limited,
Box 3293, Wellington 6001, New Zealand
Web site: www.learningmedia.com

10 9 8 7 6 5 4 3

Printed in Hong Kong

ISBN 0 478 22933 X

PL 9151

CHAPTER 1

Kelsey and Jake took grapes from the Garcias' house on the hill. They had often done it on their way home from school. The Garcias had a huge garden that stretched from the house to the street. There were lawns and flowers and trees. Instead of a front fence, there was a row of big plants with long, shiny leaves. Over the driveway, there was an arch. The grapevine grew across the arch and along two wires on posts.

Every spring, Kelsey and Jake looked at the vine on their way to school.

"I can't wait till they get ripe," Jake would say when the bunches hung like clusters of green marbles.

"It'll be ages yet," Kelsey would say. Even so, her mouth watered. She was thinking of the ripe grapes, soft and cool and as sweet as jelly.

"Grapes are my favorite fruit," Jake would say. "When I grow up, I'm going to grow rows of them all around my house."

"Yeah, so am I," Kelsey would agree.

CHAPTER 2

This fall the grapes seemed to be ripening slowly. They took ages to change from green to pink, but at last some of the bunches began to turn dark red.

"Yum! Look how many there are!" said Jake. "And we only take a few bunches."

"The Garcias have never even noticed," said Kelsey as she stared at the nearly ripe grapes. Some of the fruit glistened, as if the juice was ready to burst through the skin.

Neither of the children heard the truck coming. They jumped suddenly as the huge van honked its horn and then turned into the Garcias' driveway.

The truck driver had seen the children staring at the grapes. He grinned and shook a warning finger at them.

"He knew what we were thinking," said Kelsey. "How do grown-ups do that?"

"Who cares!" said Jake. "He doesn't know us."

"He's driving a moving van," said Kelsey. "The Garcias must be moving house."

"That's great!" said Jake. "In a couple of days the grapes will be ripe, and there'll be no one there to see how many we take."

CHAPTER 3

After school, Kelsey and Jake dared to go right into the garden. They darted between the trees and flower beds as they climbed up the hill.

"I'll bet there are things like strawberries in the garden by the house," Jake said.

"This is freaky," said Kelsey. "I don't like sneaking around."

"Why?" said Jake. "There's no one ..."
Suddenly he dived behind a tree.

"What's up? What did you see?" Kelsey's
eyes were as wide as an owl's.

"There's another truck there! They're
unloading stuff! The new
people must be there
already!"

"The new *person*,"
said a voice from
behind them.

Kelsey thought she was going to faint.
Jake's whole body froze except for his eyes,
which turned in his head toward the sound.
A tall man stepped from behind some
shrubs and came toward them. If there
hadn't been a smile under his mustache,
both children would have fled.

"Should I know you? Are you neighbors?" asked the man.

"No," Jake squeaked. He tried again. "No, we were just passing."

"Uh-huh," said the man, nodding his head. "Just passing." His smile had gone.

"We're going now," said Jake. He took a step or two backwards.

"Don't tread on my flowers, will you," said the man.

Kelsey scampered off suddenly, like a frightened rabbit. Jake raced to catch her up. Behind him, he heard the man laughing.

9

CHAPTER 4

"We'll still be able to get a bunch or two of those grapes," Jake said later.

He and Kelsey were sitting up in the huge sycamore that spread its wide arms between their two houses.

"I don't know. I thought that man was spooky," said Kelsey. "What did you say his name was?"

"Mr. Granger," said Jake. "That's what Dad told me. And he's living there alone."

Kelsey thought for a few moments. "Well, I suppose he can't watch his grapes all the time," she said. "He'll have to unpack and fix the house up and everything." She let herself go suddenly backwards to swing upside down with her knees hooked over the branch. "I'm not scared of Stranger-Granger. I'm not scared of Stranger-Granger."

"You said you were!"

"So! I'm not now." Her hair dangled and swished. "And did you see the grapes at the end of the row? They're almost black! Perfect for eating!"

11

But by the time they returned from school next afternoon, there was something new in the garden. Near the row of shiny plants and under the dangling bunches of ripening grapes, there was a sign.

CHAPTER 5

The sign said **BEWARE OF THE AGAPANTHUS**. The letters looked fierce painted in dark green on the white wood. The words sounded fierce when Kelsey and Jake said them out loud.

"Beware of the agapanthus!"

They were silent for a while, staring. Then Kelsey said, "I didn't know he had a dog."

"Is an agapanthus a dog?" asked Jake.

"It must be."

"I've never heard of an agapanthus dog." Jake was cross. "I've read books about dogs. I read *a lot* about dogs. I've never heard of an agapanthus dog!"

"Well, don't get so crabby." Kelsey glared at him. "I didn't put up the sign. So what *is* an agapanthus if it's not a dog?"

"It's probably ... Well, it's probably ..."

"Yeah? Probably what?"

Jake gave an angry kick. A stone shot across the road and whizzed into the row of shiny leaves.

"Don't do that!" hissed Kelsey. "The agapanthus might come out!" Their heads filled with thoughts of fierce teeth, claws, and angry eyes. They ran like the wind the rest of the way home.

CHAPTER 6

That night, Jake asked his older brother if he knew what an agapanthus was.

He didn't know. Kelsey asked her cousins who came to visit. They didn't know what she was talking about.

"We could ask Mom or Dad," Jake had said.

"No," said Kelsey. "You know what parents are like. They'll guess about the grapes."

"Yeah, they probably will."

The next day, they ran past Mr. Granger's garden – just in case.

"It could be something electronic," Jake puffed as they reached the school.

"Electronic?" Kelsey made a face. "I doubt it."

"It could be," said Jake. "It could be a special electronic alarm." He got excited by the idea. "If you step on the grass, it might go off! And arms will shoot out from behind trees and grab you!"

"That's stupid!" Kelsey yelled at him. But the idea scared her.

"Well, you don't know," said Jake.

"It's something fierce – with teeth!" said Kelsey. "That's what I think."

They asked some of their classmates. No one really knew. Toby Brown thought it might be a disease. April thought it was something to do with the inside of a computer.

"I said it was electronic!" said Jake after school.

"April doesn't know," Kelsey sniffed. "She just makes things up. She's always doing that."

CHAPTER 7

On Saturday, Kelsey's mother went to visit Mrs. Marshall. Kelsey went along too. After coffee, Mrs. Marshall and Kelsey's mother went outside to look at the garden. Kelsey didn't want to chat about flowers and trees. She found the pond and looked at the goldfish. Then she climbed a tree.

Down below, she could hear her mother and Mrs. Marshall talking.

"These are my new pansies," Mrs. Marshall was saying.

"They're lovely," said Kelsey's mom. "They're the very same blue as an agapanthus."

Kelsey sat up so suddenly that she nearly fell off the branch she was sitting on. An agapanthus was blue! She'd never seen a blue dog. She'd heard of blue dragons. But dragons weren't real. She was ninety-eight percent certain of that. She jumped out of the tree.

Her mother was used to her suddenly appearing, but Mrs. Marshall squealed in fright. "Sorry, Mrs. Marshall. Mom, what's an agapanthus?"

She couldn't tell Jake that night or the next day. He was away camping with his family. Sunday seemed to go on for ever. Even Monday morning before leaving for school seemed endless. But finally she and Jake were off down the road that led toward Mr. Granger's house – and the grapes that would now be just perfect for eating!

CHAPTER 8

When they got to Mr. Granger's garden, Kelsey walked across the road.

"Come on over, scaredy-cat," she called to Jake.

"But the sign is still there," said Jake.

"I know. But I'm not scared anymore." Kelsey did three fast twirls and stopped with her hands on her hips. "I know what an agapanthus is. So there!"

"What?" asked Jake. "What is it?"

"This," said Kelsey. She held onto a bunch of the long, shiny leaves that grew in clumps between the grapes and the road. "This plant is an agapanthus. Every plant in this row is an agapanthus."

Jake stared at the clumps of leaves. He knew that he had seen blue flowers growing out of them in spring.

"An agapanthus is a plant!" he said.

"We've been frightened of a plant! What could that do to us?"

"Nothing at all," said Kelsey. "Mr. Granger's sign was a trick, and we fell for it. But I'm not one bit scared anymore. And I'm going to have a bunch of those grapes right now."

Jake crossed the road. "Me too," he said. Together, they looked past the sign that said **BEWARE OF THE AGAPANTHUS**. They looked up at the grapevine that twisted over the arch and stretched out along the wires. Its leaves were still green. But in between the leaves there were no bunches of grapes! Here and there, Kelsey and Jake could see freshly cut stems. Mr. Granger had picked his grapes. There wasn't a single bunch left!

CHAPTER 9

Kelsey and Jake were so busy looking at the vine that at first they didn't hear or see Mr. Granger coming. So he seemed to just appear before them.

"Hi, kids!" he said.

His smile looked like the pretend smile you sometimes have to do for a photograph. Jake moved a few steps backwards. Kelsey moved with him. But really she wanted to stay where she was. She longed to tell Mr. Granger that she knew his sign was a trick and that they weren't fooled by it anymore.

"Looking at the grapevine, were you?" Mr. Granger asked. "I was very pleased with all the grapes I picked. A great crop." He waved his arm, and the children saw that he was holding a large hammer. They watched him walk to the sign. With just a few taps, he loosened the sign and tucked it under his arm.

"I put this here, just in the meantime, to keep little children away." He smiled again, but Kelsey still didn't like it. He seemed to be laughing at them. "I don't want children in my garden."

"Only little children would be scared by that sign," she said. "We know that an agapanthus is a plant. Come on, Jake. We'll be late for school."

"See ya, kids."

As they hurried up the road, Jake growled at Kelsey. "Why did you tell him we knew about the agapanthus? He would have thought we were scared, but next year we could have got the grapes anyway. He wouldn't have known."

Kelsey scowled. "Rats. I never thought of that!"

"Well, you should have," Jake said crossly.

"Anyway," said Kelsey with a sniff, "I'm going to walk on his lawn. It's right by the road, and he can't stop me."

CHAPTER 10

After school, Kelsey stalked down the road. She hadn't forgotten what she had said that morning. "Hurry up, slowpoke," she called behind her to Jake. Quite a way from Mr. Granger's garden, Jake called out, "He's put the sign up again. I can see it."

"So! We're not scared of that."

But, as they came closer to the garden, they saw that it wasn't the same sign at all. It was a new one. It was in a different place. It was white like the last one had been, but the board with the writing on was longer and narrower. The writing said **A GIANT SCHNAUZER PATROLS THIS PROPERTY**.

Kelsey laughed out loud. "He thinks he can trick us again! A giant … whatever it is … is probably some sort of daisy! Flowers don't walk around. That's what 'patrols' means, doesn't it?"

Jake said something, but his voice seemed rather far away, and Kelsey couldn't hear it. "What did you say, Jake?"

"Come over here!"

Kelsey turned round. Jake was across the road. "You don't need to be scared of a flower this time," he said. "It's not a flower. A schnauzer is a dog! It's a *huge* dog!"

Kelsey stood for a moment on the edge of Mr. Granger's lawn. She was remembering how Jake loved reading dog books. He knew everything about dogs. She looked up toward the house but couldn't see anything moving.

"A giant schnauzer is real big!" Jake
called.

Kelsey walked backwards for a while,
looking at Mr. Granger's house. "You
know," she said, "I think that sign is
another trick. He probably hasn't got a dog
at all."

"I'm not going to be the one to find out,"
said Jake. Then he stopped suddenly. "Did
you hear that?"

"Hear what?"

"I thought I heard a dog barking,"
he said.

"He's won, hasn't he?" said Kelsey.

"This time," said Jake. "But who cares? When I grow up, I'm growing my own grapes, and I'm having a garden twice as big as Stranger-Granger's – and six friendly dogs in it."

"Me too," said Kelsey.